W9-CDF-153

READY for ANYTHING!

KEIKO KASZA

SCHOLASTIC INC.
New York Toronto London Auckland
Sydney Mexico City New Delhi Hong Kong

To Mr. Uraki at Saera Shobou
who believed in me first.

No part of this publication may be reproduced, stored in a retrieval system, or transmitted in any form or by any means, electronic, mechanical, photocopying, recording, or otherwise, without written permission of the publisher. For information regarding permission, write to G. P. Putnam's Sons, a division of Penguin Young Readers Group, a member of Penguin Group (USA) Inc., 345 Hudson Street, New York, NY 10014.

ISBN 978-0-545-34272-8

Copyright © 2009 by Keiko Kasza.
All rights reserved. Published by Scholastic Inc., 557 Broadway, New York, NY 10012, by arrangement with G. P. Putnam's Sons, a division of Penguin Young Readers Group, a member of Penguin Group (USA) Inc. SCHOLASTIC and associated logos are trademarks and/or registered trademarks of Scholastic Inc.

12 11 10 9 8 7 6 5 4 3 2 1   11 12 13 14 15 16/0

Printed in the U.S.A.   08

First Scholastic printing, January 2011

Design by Marikka Tamura
Text set in Greco
The art was done in gouache on three-ply bristol illustration paper.

Duck arrived at
Raccoon's house on
a bright, sunny day.

"Hey, Raccoon!" said Duck. "Are you ready for our picnic?"

"Umm, well . . . I changed my mind," said Raccoon. "I don't want to go."

"Why not?" asked Duck.

"Well, I've been thinking," said Raccoon. "What if we are attacked by killer bees?"

"No . . . ," said Duck.

"Yeah," said Raccoon. "And what if they chase us, you know, and we fall into a river?"

"Oh, no," cried Duck.

"Oh, yeah," said Raccoon. "And what if we swim for our lives, but a terrible storm strikes?"

"Oh, no! Oh, no!" yelled Duck.

"Oh, yeah! Oh, yeah!" Raccoon went on. "And what if we look for shelter in a cave, but there's already someone in there, someone really scary?"

"Like . . . like who?" asked Duck.

"A DRAGON!!!!!"

shouted Raccoon.

"AAAAAaaa!"

They both screamed . . .

. . . and they hid under a blanket.
"It could happen, you know," Raccoon warned.
"Picnics are dangerous."

"You're right." Duck thought about it for a while.
"But Raccoon . . .

. . . what if some lovely butterflies pass by instead of bees?"

"Hmm, that would be nice," said Raccoon.

"Yes," said Duck. "And what if we follow the butterflies to the river and jump in for a cool splash?"

"That would be even nicer,"
Raccoon answered.

"Yes, much nicer," Duck said. "And what if the weather is beautiful, with just a gentle breeze blowing? We could fly a kite!"

"Gee, that sounds like fun!" Raccoon admitted.

"Lots of fun!" Duck said. "And then,
we might find a cave to explore."

"Don't go in!" Raccoon shouted. "There's
a fire-breathing dragon in there! Remember?"

"Maybe," said Duck. "But what if it's just a cute little dragon who wants to play with us?"

"You think?" said Raccoon.

"Sure," said Duck. "And what if we have
the best picnic ever, roasting marshmallows?"

"Wow!" said Raccoon. "Your what-ifs
are wonderful, Duck."

"What are we waiting for?" Raccoon cried.
"Let's go on a picnic!"

"That's the spirit, Raccoon!" Duck cheered.

"Just give me a few minutes to get ready,"
said Raccoon.

So Duck waited . . .

And waited . . .

And waited
some more . . .

Until finally
Raccoon announced,
"Okay, Duck,
I'm ready to go!"

"Oh, Raccoon." Duck fell over, laughing.
"You worry too much. But I guess you
are ready for anything, huh?"

At last the two friends left for their picnic.
"Thanks, Duck," said Raccoon. "This is much
more fun than hiding under a blanket."

"No problem," said Duck. "Trust me. Nothing
could go wrong on a little picnic."

But when they got there . . . Duck gasped!
"**OH, NO!**" Duck moaned. "**I FORGOT
THE PICNIC BASKET!**"

Duck wanted to cry, but Raccoon stayed calm.

"No problem," Raccoon declared, opening his backpack.

"Like you said . . .